MW01489953

Little Red-Cap
Rotkäppchen

Bilingual Edition: English – German
Zweisprachige Ausgabe: Englisch – Deutsch

Brothers Grimm
Brüder Grimm

ISBN-13: 9781521029138

Table of Contents
Inhaltsverzeichnis

Little Red-Cap 1

Rotkäppchen 7

Little Red-Cap

Once upon a time there was a dear little girl who was loved by every one who looked at her, but most of all by her grandmother, and there was nothing that she would not have given to the child. Once she gave her a little cap of red velvet, which suited her so well that she would never wear anything else; so she was always called 'Little Red-Cap.'

One day her mother said to her, "Come, Little Red-Cap, here is a piece of cake and a bottle of wine; take them to your grandmother, she is ill and weak, and they will do her good. Set out before it gets hot, and when you are going, walk nicely and quietly and do not run off the path, or you may fall and break the bottle, and then your grandmother will get nothing; and when you go into her room, don't forget to say, 'Good-morning,' and don't peep into every corner before you do it."

"I will take great care," said Little Red-Cap to her mother, and gave her hand on it.

The grandmother lived out in the wood, half a league from the village, and just as Little Red-Cap entered the wood, a wolf met her. Red-Cap did not know what a wicked creature he was, and was not at all afraid of him.

"Good-day, Little Red-Cap," said he.

"Thank you kindly, wolf"

"Whither away so early, Little Red-Cap?"

"To my grandmother's."

"What have you got in your apron?"

"Cake and wine; yesterday was baking-day, so poor sick grandmother is to have something good, to make her stronger."

"Where does your grandmother live, Little Red-Cap?"

"A good quarter of a league farther on in the wood; her house stands under the three large oak-trees, the nut-trees are just below; you surely must know it," replied Little Red-Cap.

The wolf thought to himself, "What a tender young creature! what a nice plump mouthful—she will be better to eat than the old woman. I must act craftily, so as to catch both." So he walked for a short time by the side of Little Red-Cap, and then he said, "See, Little Red-Cap, how pretty the flowers are about here—why do you not look round? I believe, too, that you do not hear how sweetly the little birds are singing; you walk gravely along as if you were going to school, while everything else out here in the wood is merry."

Little Red-Cap raised her eyes, and when she saw the sunbeams dancing here and there through the trees, and pretty flowers growing everywhere, she thought, "Suppose I take grandmother a fresh nosegay; that would please her too. It is so early in the day that I shall still get there in good time;" and so she ran from the path into the wood to look for flowers. And whenever she had picked one, she fancied that she saw a still prettier one farther on, and ran after it, and so got deeper and deeper into the wood.

Meanwhile the wolf ran straight to the grandmother's house and knocked at the door.

"Who is there?"

"Little Red-Cap," replied the wolf. "She is bringing cake and wine; open the door."

"Lift the latch," called out the grandmother, "I am too weak, and cannot get up."

The wolf lifted the latch, the door flew open, and without saying a word he went straight to the grandmother's bed, and devoured her. Then he put on her clothes, dressed himself in her cap, laid himself in bed and drew the curtains.

Little Red-Cap, however, had been running about picking flowers, and when she had gathered so many that she could carry no more, she remembered her grandmother, and set out on the way to her.

She was surprised to find the cottage-door standing open, and when she went into the room, she had such a strange feeling that she said to herself, "Oh dear! how uneasy I feel to-day, and at other times I like being with grandmother so much." She called out, "Good morning," but received no answer; so she went to the bed and drew back the curtains. There lay her grandmother with her cap pulled far over her face, and looking very strange.

"Oh! grandmother," she said, "what big ears you have!"

"The better to hear you with, my child," was the reply.

"But, grandmother, what big eyes you have!" she said.

"The better to see you with, my dear."

"But, grandmother, what large hands you have!"

"The better to hug you with."

"Oh! but, grandmother, what a terrible big mouth you have!"

"The better to eat you with!"

And scarcely had the wolf said this, than with one bound he was out of bed and swallowed up Red-Cap.

When the wolf had appeased his appetite, he lay down again in the bed, fell asleep and began to snore very loud. The huntsman was just passing the house, and thought to himself, "How the old woman is snoring! I must just see if she wants anything." So he went into the room, and when he came to the bed, he saw that the wolf was lying in it. "Do I find thee here, thou old sinner!" said he. "I have long sought thee!" Then just as he was going to fire at him, it occurred to him that the wolf might have devoured the grandmother, and that she might still be saved, so he did not fire, but took a pair of scissors, and began to cut open the stomach of the sleeping wolf. When he had made two snips, he saw the little Red-Cap shining, and then he made two snips more, and the little girl sprang out, crying, "Ah, how frightened I have been! How dark it was inside the wolf;" and after that the aged grandmother came out alive also, but scarcely able to breathe. Red-Cap, however, quickly fetched great stones with which they filled the wolf's body, and when he awoke, he wanted to run away, but the stones were so heavy that he fell down at once, and fell dead.

Then all three were delighted. The huntsman drew off the wolf's skin and went home with it; the grandmother ate the cake and drank the wine which Red-Cap had brought, and revived, but Red-Cap thought to herself, "As long as I live, I will never by myself leave the path, to run into the wood, when my mother has forbidden me to do so."

It is also related that once when Red-Cap was again taking cakes to the old grandmother, another wolf spoke to her, and tried to entice her from the path. Red-Cap was, however, on her guard, and went straight forward on her way, and told her grandmother that she had met the wolf, and that he had said "good-morning" to her, but with such a wicked look in his eyes, that if they had not been on the public road she was certain he would have eaten her up. "Well," said the grandmother, "we will shut the door, that he may not come in." Soon afterwards the wolf knocked, and cried, "Open the door, grandmother, I am little Red-Cap, and am fetching you some cakes." But they did not speak, or open the door, so the grey-beard stole twice or thrice round the house, and at last jumped on the roof, intending to wait until Red-Cap went home in the evening, and then to steal after her and devour her in the darkness. But the grandmother saw what was in his thoughts. In front of the house was a great stone trough, so she said to the child, "Take the pail, Red-Cap; I made some sausages yesterday, so carry the water in which I boiled them to the trough." Red-Cap carried until the great trough was quite full. Then the smell of the sausages reached the wolf, and he sniffed and peeped down, and at last stretched out his neck so far that he could no longer keep his footing and began to slip, and slipped down from the roof straight into the great trough, and was drowned. But Red-Cap went joyously home, and never did anything to harm any one.

Rotkäppchen

Es war einmal eine kleine süße Dirne, die hatte jedermann lieb, der sie nur ansah, am allerliebsten aber ihre Großmutter, die wußte gar nicht was sie alles dem Kinde geben sollte. Einmal schenkte sie ihm ein Käppchen von rotem Sammet und weil ihm das so wohl stand, und es nichts anderes mehr tragen wollte, hieß es nur das Rotkäppchen. Eines Tages sprach seine Mutter zu ihm: »Komm, Rotkäppchen, da hast du ein Stück Kuchen und eine Flasche Wein, bring das der Großmutter hinaus; sie ist krank und schwach und wird sich daran laben. Mach dich auf, bevor es heiß wird, und wenn du hinauskommst, so geh hübsch sittsam und lauf nicht vom Weg ab, sonst fällst du und zerbrichst das Glas und die Großmutter hat nichts. Und wenn du in ihre Stube kommst, so vergiß nicht guten Morgen zu sagen und guck nicht erst in alle Ecken herum.«

»Ich will schon alles gut machen,« sagte Rotkäppchen zur Mutter, und gab ihr die Hand darauf. Die Großmutter aber wohnte draußen im Wald, eine halbe Stunde vom Dorf. Wie nun Rotkäppchen in den Wald kam, begegnete ihm der Wolf. Rotkäppchen aber wußte nicht was das für ein böses Tier war und fürchtete sich nicht vor ihm. »Guten Tag, Rotkäppchen,« sprach er. »Schönen Dank, Wolf.« »Wohinaus so früh, Rotkäppchen?« »Zur Großmutter.« »Was trägst du unter der Schürze?« »Kuchen und Wein, gestern haben wir gebacken, da soll sich die kranke und schwache Großmutter etwas zu gute thun und sich damit stärken.« »Rotkäppchen, wo wohnt deine Großmutter?« »Noch eine gute Viertelstunde weiter im Wald, unter den drei großen Eichbäumen, da steht ihr Haus, unten sind die Nußhecken, das wirst du ja wissen,« sagte Rotkäppchen. Der Wolf dachte bei sich: »Das junge zarte Ding, das ist ein fetter Bissen, der wird noch besser schmecken als die Alte; du mußt es listig anfangen, damit du beide erschnappst.« Da ging er ein Weilchen neben Rotkäppchen her, dann sprach er: »Rotkäppchen, sieh einmal die schönen Blumen, die ringsumher stehen, warum guckst du dich nicht um? ich glaube du hörst gar nicht, wie die Vöglein so lieblich singen? du gehst ja für dich hin als wenn du zur Schule gingst, und ist so lustig haußen in dem Wald.«

Rotkäppchen schlug die Augen auf, und als es sah wie die Sonnenstrahlen durch die Bäume hin und her tanzten, und alles voll schöner Blumen stand, dachte es: »Wenn ich der Großmutter einen frischen Strauß mitbringe, der wird ihr auch Freude machen: es ist so früh am Tage, daß ich doch zu rechter Zeit ankomme,« lief vom Wege ab in den Wald hinein und suchte Blumen. Und wenn es eine gebrochen hatte, meinte es, weiter hinaus stände eine schönere, und lief danach, und geriet immer tiefer in den Wald hinein. Der Wolf aber ging geradeswegs nach dem Hause der Großmutter und klopfte an die Thür. »Wer ist draußen?« »Rotkäppchen, das bringt Kuchen und Wein, mach auf.« »Drück nur auf die Klinke,« rief die Großmutter, »ich bin zu schwach und kann nicht aufstehen.« Der Wolf drückte auf die Klinke, die Thür sprang auf und er ging, ohne ein Wort zu sprechen, gerade zum Bett der Großmutter und verschluckte sie. Dann that er ihre Kleider an, setzte ihre Haube auf, legte sich in ihr Bett und zog die Vorhänge vor.

Rotkäppchen aber war nach den Blumen herumgelaufen, und als es so viel zusammen hatte, daß es keine mehr tragen konnte, fiel ihm die Großmutter wieder ein und es machte sich auf den Weg zu ihr. Es wunderte sich, daß die Thür aufstand, und wie es in die Stube trat, so kam es ihm so seltsam darin vor, daß es dachte: »Ei, du mein Gott, wie ängstlich wird mir's heute zu Mut, und bin sonst so gern bei der Großmutter!« Es rief: »Guten Morgen,« bekam aber keine Antwort. Darauf ging es zum Bett und zog die Vorhänge zurück; da lag die Großmutter, und hatte die Haube tief ins Gesicht gesetzt und sah so wunderlich aus. »Ei, Großmutter, was hast du für große Ohren!« »Daß ich dich besser hören kann.« »Ei, Großmutter, was hast du für große Augen!« »Daß ich dich besser sehen kann.« »Ei, Großmutter, was hast du für große Hände!« »Daß ich dich besser packen kann.« »Aber, Großmutter, was hast du für ein entsetzlich großes Maul!« »Daß ich dich besser fressen kann.« Kaum hatte der Wolf das gesagt, so that er einen Satz aus dem Bett und verschlang das arme Rotkäppchen.

Wie der Wolf sein Gelüsten gestillt hatte, legte er sich wieder ins Bett, schlief ein und fing an überlaut zu schnarchen. Der Jäger ging eben an dem Hause vorbei und dachte: »Wie die alte Frau schnarcht, du mußt doch sehen, ob ihr etwas fehlt.«

Da trat er in die Stube, und wie er vor das Bett kam, so sah er, daß der Wolf darin lag. »Finde ich dich hier, du alter Sünder,« sagte er, »ich habe dich lange gesucht.« Nun wollte er seine Büchse anlegen, da fiel ihm ein, der Wolf könnte die Großmutter gefressen haben, und sie wäre noch zu retten; schoß nicht, sondern nahm eine Schere und fing an dem schlafenden Wolf den Bauch aufzuschneiden. Wie er ein paar Schnitte gethan hatte, da sah er das rote Käppchen leuchten, und noch ein paar Schnitte, da sprang das Mädchen heraus und rief: »Ach, wie war ich erschrocken, wie war's so dunkel in dem Wolf seinem Leib!« Und dann kam die alte Großmutter auch noch lebendig heraus und konnte kaum atmen. Rotkäppchen aber holte geschwind große Steine, damit füllten sie dem Wolf den Leib, und wie er aufwachte, wollte er fortspringen, aber die Steine waren so schwer, daß er gleich niedersank und sich totfiel.

Da waren alle drei vergnügt; der Jäger zog dem Wolf den Pelz ab und ging damit heim, die Großmutter aß den Kuchen und trank den Wein, den Rotkäppchen gebracht hatte, und erholte sich wieder, Rotkäppchen aber dachte: »Du willst dein Lebtag nicht wieder allein vom Wege ab in den Wald laufen, wenn dir's die Mutter verboten hat.«

Es wird auch erzählt, daß einmal, als Rotkäppchen der alten Großmutter wieder Gebackenes brachte, ein anderer Wolf ihm zugesprochen und es vom Wege habe ableiten wollen. Rotkäppchen aber hütete sich und ging gerade fort seines Wegs und sagte der Großmutter, daß es dem Wolf begegnet wäre, der ihm guten Tag gewünscht, aber so bös aus den Augen geguckt hätte: »Wenn's nicht auf offener Straße gewesen wäre, er hätte mich gefressen.« »Komm,« sagte die Großmutter, »wir wollen die Thür verschließen, daß er nicht herein kann.« Bald danach klopfte der Wolf an und rief: »Mach auf, Großmutter,

ich bin das Rotkäppchen, ich bring dir Gebackenes.«
Sie schwiegen aber still und machten die Thür nicht
auf; da schlich der Graukopf etliche Male um das
Haus, sprang endlich aufs Dach und wollte warten bis
Rotkäppchen abends nach Haus ginge, dann wollte er
ihm nachschleichen und wollt's in der Dunkelheit
fressen. Aber die Großmutter merkte, was er im Sinn
hatte. Nun stand vor dem Hause ein großer Steintrog,
da sprach sie zu dem Kinde: »Nimm den Eimer,
Rotkäppchen, gestern habe ich Würste gekocht, da
trag das Wasser, worin sie gekocht sind, in den Trog.«
Rotkäppchen trug so lange, bis der große, große Trog
ganz voll war. Da stieg der Geruch von den Würsten
dem Wolf in die Nase, er schnupperte und guckte
hinab, endlich machte er den Hals so lang, daß er sich
nicht mehr halten konnte und anfing zu rutschen; so
rutschte er vom Dach herab, gerade in den großen
Trog hinein und ertrank. Rotkäppchen aber ging
fröhlich nach Haus, und that ihm niemand etwas
zuleide.

LITTLE RED-CAP / ROTKÄPPCHEN

LITTLE RED-CAP / ROTKÄPPCHEN

LITTLE RED-CAP / ROTKÄPPCHEN

LITTLE RED-CAP / ROTKÄPPCHEN

BROTHERS GRIMM / BRÜDER GRIMM

Made in United States
North Haven, CT
13 January 2022

14696074R00015